FROM mommy

This book belongs to

Emilio Duran

1010610i

BOUGHT OCT. 6-01

DISNEY·PIXAR

MONSTERS, INC.

A READ-ALOUD STORYBOOK

Adapted by Catherine Hapka
Illustrated by the Disney Storybook Artists

Designed by Disney's Global Design Group

Random House 🏠 New York

Copyright © 2001 by Disney Enterprises, Inc./Pixar Animation Studios. All rights reserved under International and Pan-American Copyright Conventions. Published in the United States by Random House, Inc., New York, and simultaneously in Canada by Random House of Canada Limited, Toronto, in conjunction with Disney Enterprises, Inc. RANDOM HOUSE and colophon are registered trademarks of Random House, Inc. Library of Congress Control Number: 2001089024 ISBN: 0-7364-1235-2

Printed in the United States of America
October 2001
10 9 8 7 6 5 4 3 2 1

www.randomhouse.com/kids/disney

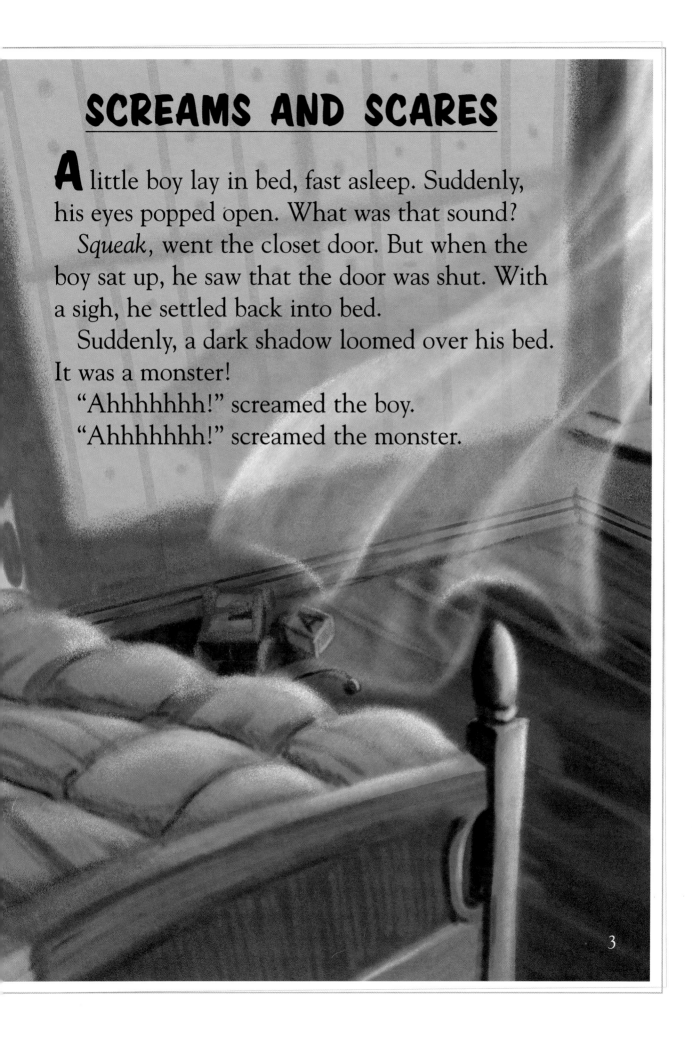

SCREAMS AND SCARES

A little boy lay in bed, fast asleep. Suddenly, his eyes popped open. What was that sound?

Squeak, went the closet door. But when the boy sat up, he saw that the door was shut. With a sigh, he settled back into bed.

Suddenly, a dark shadow loomed over his bed. It was a monster!

"Ahhhhhhh!" screamed the boy.

"Ahhhhhhh!" screamed the monster.

Lights flashed. The little boy and his room weren't real after all. This was a training room at Monsters, Inc.—where new employees learned to be Scarers.

Ms. Flint, the instructor, was clearly unhappy. She pointed to the closet door. "Leaving a door open is the worst mistake any employee can make, because . . . ?"

". . . it could let in a child!" Mr. Waternoose, the CEO of Monsters, Inc., finished the sentence.

Monsters thought children and even their toys and clothes were very dangerous.

Still, monsters needed kids because their screams made energy. So every night, Scarers entered the human world through kids' closet doors to collect scream energy. It was a risky job.

Waternoose sighed. These new Scarers needed a *lot* of help.

Meanwhile, top Scarer James P. Sullivan and his friend and assistant, Mike Wazowski, were on their way to work. Mike stopped in front of his car.

"Okay, Sulley, hop on in," Mike said.

"Nope," Sulley replied. "There's a scream shortage." Mike's car ran on scream fuel, and monsters were collecting fewer screams than ever before.

When they walked into Monsters, Inc., Mike stopped to chat with his girlfriend, Celia. It was her birthday, so he told her he was going to take her to dinner at her favorite restaurant.

"I'll see you at 5:01 and not a minute later," Mike said before heading to the locker room.

As Mike sat by his locker getting ready for work, a creepy monster oozed out of the shadows.

"Wazowski!" the monster said mockingly. Mike shrieked. It was Randall, another Scarer and Sulley's biggest rival.

"I'm in the zone today," Randall bragged. "Going to be doing some serious scaring."

Mike wasn't worried about Randall beating Sulley's record. But he *was* worried about Roz getting annoyed with him. Roz was the monster in charge of paperwork, and Mike was sometimes careless about turning in his reports.

"I'm watching you, Wazowski," Roz warned sternly as Mike hurried past her.

When he reached the Scare Floor, Mike joined the
other assistants. Then the Scarers, including Sulley,
arrived and started getting ready for the day's work.

Soon the Scarers started jumping in and out of doors, collecting screams. Sulley and Mike were having a great day. Sulley even captured a big bunch of screams at a slumber party! But not everyone had such good luck.

One monster returned in shock from a child's door. He had failed to scare the child inside. That door was quickly shredded. A kid who wasn't afraid of monsters simply wouldn't provide any scream energy.

"Kids these days. They just don't get scared like they used to," Waternoose mumbled as he watched.

Suddenly, a Scarer named George emerged from a door. He had a child's sock stuck to his back!

"Twenty-three-nineteen!" his assistant screamed.

Alarms sounded! Agents from the CDA—the Child Detection Agency—rushed to decontaminate George and blow up the toxic sock.

At the end of the day, Mike was getting ready to meet Celia when he realized something. "Oh, no! My scare reports—I left them on my desk!" he cried.

Sulley offered to take care of the paperwork so Mike wouldn't be late for his date.

But when Sulley walked back onto the empty Scare Floor, he noticed something odd: one kid's door hadn't been put away.

Sulley peeked warily through the door. "Hello? Is anybody scaring in here?"

BOO!

As Sulley turned to leave, he heard a THUMP. He turned around and saw . . . a little girl clinging to his tail!

"Aaaaaaaah!" he screamed in terror. The kid was touching him!

The girl giggled. "Kitty!" she said to the big, furry monster.

21

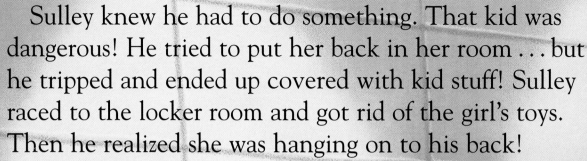

Sulley knew he had to do something. That kid was dangerous! He tried to put her back in her room ... but he tripped and ended up covered with kid stuff! Sulley raced to the locker room and got rid of the girl's toys. Then he realized she was hanging on to his back!

Sulley put the girl in a gym bag and ran back to the Scare Floor. Just then, Randall showed up! Sulley hid and watched in horror as Randall sent the kid's door to the vault. Now how could Sulley put the girl back in her room?

23

Meanwhile, Mike and Celia were enjoying
a romantic meal. "You know, I was just thinking
about the first time I laid eye on you—how
pretty you looked," Mike cooed.

Just then, Sulley appeared at the window!

Sulley came inside and sat down. "Hi, guys," he
said, setting his bag under the table. "Look in the
bag!" he whispered to Mike.

When Mike looked, the bag wasn't there.

"Aaaaah!" someone yelled from across the restaurant. "A kid! A human kid!"

"Boo!" a voice cried with a giggle.

Sulley gasped. It was the girl! He tried to grab her as everyone in the restaurant screamed and ran for the exits.

27

Within minutes, the CDA swarmed the restaurant. Mike wanted to get to Celia, but he needed to help Sulley sneak away with the girl.

Back at home, they tried to figure out what to do. They dressed in protective gear to stay safe from the girl as she happily explored the apartment. They were terrified of her! When she cried, the lights flashed. When she laughed, they flashed even brighter!

Finally, the girl got tired and climbed into Sulley's bed. But she wouldn't go to sleep. She pointed to the closet door and showed Sulley a picture she had drawn.

"Hey, that looks like Randall," Sulley said. Suddenly, he understood—Randall was the girl's assigned monster. She was scared of him! To comfort her, Sulley showed her that the closet was empty. No monsters there!

When the girl finally fell asleep, Sulley watched her for a few moments. She didn't look very dangerous at all.

The next day, Sulley and Mike disguised the girl as a monster child and returned to Monsters, Inc. They hoped to find her door and send her home before anyone found out she was there. But the company was crawling with CDA agents!

"Don't panic," Sulley whispered to Mike when Waternoose stopped them in the lobby.

Sulley made his way to the locker room with Mike and the girl.

Then Mike raced off to find the card key for the girl's door. Sulley played with her while they waited.

"Boo!" the girl cried happily as she ran around, playing hide-and-seek.

Just as Mike returned, Randall entered the men's room. The friends hid while Randall asked his assistant, Fungus, about the girl and said something about a machine.

"What were they talking about?" Sulley wondered aloud after Randall left. But there was no time to think about it. He and Mike had to get the girl back through her door right away!

37

None of the other monsters noticed that anything was wrong as Mike and Sulley took the girl to the Scare Floor. But there was a problem—Mike had the wrong card key!

"Mike, this isn't Boo's door," Sulley protested. Mike was shocked that Sulley had named the girl. "Once you name it, you start getting attached to it!" he exclaimed.

While they bickered, Boo slipped away!

Sulley and Mike looked everywhere for Boo. Suddenly, Celia appeared and cornered Mike. She was very angry about their ruined dinner. Randall overheard them and grinned. He realized Mike had been at the restaurant and must know about the kid!

Once Celia had left, Randall grabbed Mike. He told him to bring Boo to the Scare Floor during lunch, when everyone else would be gone, and he would have her door.

Sulley was still looking for Boo when he spotted a piece of her costume in the trash compactor. Tearfully, Sulley picked up the cube of trash, fearing the worst. Just then he heard a familiar voice. Boo was alive! She was with a group of monster kids.

"Kitty!" Boo called when she saw Sulley. She giggled, which made the lights flicker and pop. The other monsters in the hall cried out in fright. Sulley had to get Boo back to her door!

RANDALL'S SECRET

"Come on!" cried Mike, leading Sulley and Boo to the Scare Floor.

When they got there, Mike raced right over to Boo's door.

"There it is!" Mike cried. "Just like Randall said!" But Sulley didn't trust Randall, so Mike jumped onto the bed to prove it was safe.

Sulley watched in horror as someone caught Mike in a trap. It was Randall!

Thinking he had trapped Boo, Randall raced off with the box. Now Sulley had to rescue Mike! He and Boo followed Randall through a hidden door.

There they discovered Randall's terrible secret. He had created a giant machine to capture scream energy. He wanted to use Boo and other human children to test it! Mike was already in the chair, and Randall was going to turn it on at any moment.

46

Sulley managed to rescue Mike from Randall. "Follow me!" Sulley cried. "I have an idea!"

Sulley went straight to Waternoose, the most trusted monster at Monsters, Inc., to get some help. Waternoose was shocked to see Boo.

"It's not our fault—it's Randall's!" Mike told Waternoose while Sulley tried to comfort a frightened Boo.

But Waternoose already knew all about Randall's evil scheme! He quickly grabbed Boo. Then, with Randall's help, he banished Sulley and Mike to a snowy wasteland in the human world by pushing them through a one-way door.

There Sulley and Mike met the Abominable Snowman. He had been banished years ago. Sulley was able to use some supplies from his cave to make a sled. Sulley offered Mike a ride, but Mike refused, blaming him for the mess they were in.

On his own, Sulley found his way to a human
village and burst back into the monster world through
a child's closet door. He reached Randall's machine
just in time to see Boo being strapped into it.

"Kitty!" Boo cried as soon as she saw Sulley.

Sulley smashed the machine and grabbed the
little girl.

As Sulley escaped with Boo, Mike suddenly caught up with them. He had realized he was angry with Sulley—but not angry enough to lose his friend.

Together they raced to the Scare Floor, with Randall in hot pursuit. When a crowd of monsters got in Randall's way, Sulley, Mike, and Boo jumped onto the door conveyor system and tried to make their way toward Boo's door.

But her door kept moving away from them. The friends simply needed more power to help them reach Boo's door. Sulley had an idea.

He asked Mike to make Boo laugh. Her laughter created enough energy to power up all the doors. Sulley and Mike took Boo and ran. Randall chased them in and out of kids' closet doors all over the world! Finally, Mike and Sulley managed to kick Randall through a door and smash it. Randall was gone for good.

But now Waternoose was after them! While Mike distracted the CDA, Sulley took Boo and ran. Waternoose chased them right through Boo's door into her room.

Sulley tried to convince Waternoose to let Boo go. But Waternoose refused. He said he'd bring a thousand kids into the monster world to end the scream shortage and save Monsters, Inc.

Little did he know he was really in the Scarers' training room! The CDA was watching, and Mike had taped every shocking word Waternoose had said.

The friends learned that the CDA had been investigating Monsters, Inc., for years! And the head of the investigation was—Roz! Roz gave Sulley some time to tuck Boo into her own bed. Sulley knew that Boo would be safe. But he also knew that her door would be shredded and he'd never see her again.

"Good-bye, Boo," he said softly as he turned to leave.

From that day on, Monsters, Inc., was a different company. As Sulley had discovered, kids' laughter was much more powerful than their screams. Instead of scaring children, the monsters made them laugh. The energy crisis was over!

Mike became one of the top Laugh Collectors, and Sulley was the company's new president. But he still missed Boo.

Then one day, Mike surprised him—he'd rebuilt Boo's door so Sulley could visit her!

"Boo?"
"Kitty!"